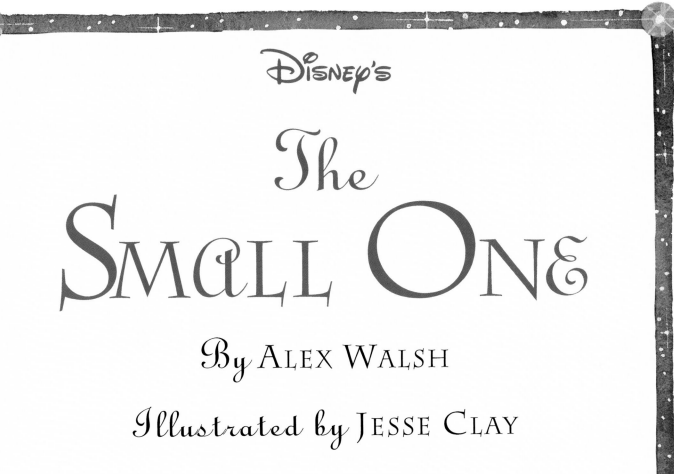

Disney's
The
SMALL ONE

By ALEX WALSH

Illustrated by JESSE CLAY

SCHOLASTIC INC.
New York Toronto London Auckland Sydney

ISBN 0-590-13765-4

12 11 10 9 8 7 6 5 4 3 2 1   6 7 8 9/9 0 1/0

Printed in the U.S.A.   37

First Scholastic printing, November 1996

The artwork for each picture is prepared using watercolors.
This book is set in 14-point Hiroshige Book.
Designed by Yolanda Monteza.

"I don't know exactly how *Small One* came into our lives. I just remember my son Cody introducing it to me one night and loving every moment of it. As a mother I am constantly on my guard about what my children eat, think, watch, say, and do. We live in a violent, often selfish world where 'sentimental' is deemed corny and 'spiritual' means ignorant. We seem to have lost our heart. But *Small One* reminds us that 'there is no greater love than being willing to lay down one's life for a friend.' What a wonderful message for today's world—and for today's children. Cody and I are delighted to introduce you to what will become a lifelong friend—*Small One*."

—*Kathie Lee Gifford*

February 22, 1995

New York

Before honor is humility.
—*Proverbs* 15:33

O*nce* long ago there was a little boy who lived outside a town called Nazareth. His father owned four donkeys. Three of the donkeys were young and strong. The fourth donkey was old and weak. But the boy loved him best of all. The donkey's name was Small One.

Each day the boy brought food and water to all the donkeys.
But Small One was the only donkey he played with. Small One was
his friend.

One day the boy was going to help his father gather firewood.
"Are the donkeys ready yet?" his father called.

The boy was feeding Small One. "Almost, Father," he replied.
"Hurry up," he said to the little donkey.

The boy and his father took the four donkeys and went over the
hills to gather firewood. The father walked in front with the three
strong donkeys. The boy walked behind, leading Small One. As they
went about their work, the boy tried to find the lightest pieces of
wood. He knew that Small One was too old and weak to carry a
heavy load.

Meanwhile, the boy's father was putting heavy pieces of wood onto the backs of the other three donkeys. He saw that his son was putting only little sticks on Small One's back. He did not like it, but he said nothing.

When it was time to go home, the boy pushed Small One up a hill. The little donkey was very tired.

All of a sudden there was a crash!

Small One had slipped down the hill and dropped the firewood. The boy hurried to pick up the wood. He put a few pieces on Small One's back and carried the rest himself.

When the boy reached the top of the hill with the little donkey, his father was waiting for him. He was angry.

"Don't you have enough work to do without doing Small One's, too?" he said.

"Oh, Father . . . he is no trouble at all. I don't mind," said the boy.

As they walked home, the father spoke to the boy. "Son, Small One can no longer carry a load big enough to pay for his food."

The boy put his arms around Small One's neck.

"He is just a little tired today, Father," he said. "His strength will come back."

"No, he is old, my son. His strength is gone. We cannot afford to keep him any longer."

The boy grabbed his father's arm. "No, Father . . . you don't mean that!"

The father put his arms around the boy.

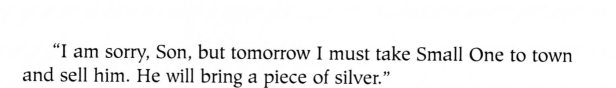

"I am sorry, Son, but tomorrow I must take Small One to town and sell him. He will bring a piece of silver."

The boy began to cry.

"No, Father, no!" he said. "You can't sell him. You *can't!*"

"Please, Son, try to understand," said his father. "Small One is old. He should not have to work so hard. In town he will have an

easier life. You must be strong."

As his father turned away, the boy said quietly, "May I take him to town?"

"Very well," said his father. "You can leave in the morning and be home by nightfall. But understand . . . Small One *must* be sold."

"Yes, Father," the boy replied sadly.

After his father left, the boy talked to his little donkey. "Don't worry, Small One. You won't have to carry these heavy sticks anymore. And I won't sell you to just anyone. He will be someone special, someone who will feed you and brush your coat and love you as I do."

The little donkey was very sad.

"Somewhere there is a special friend for you," the boy went on. "And somehow we will find him."

The donkey licked the boy on the nose.

"Good night, Small One," said the boy as he covered the donkey up for the night.

The next day the boy and Small One walked over the hills to town. Soon they came to the town gates. The town was a very busy place. The boy and the donkey felt very small amid the legs of tall horses and camels and the wheels of many carts.

At the gates the boy and Small One were stopped by a guard. "What do you want, boy?" he asked.

"I have come to sell my donkey, sir," said the boy.

The guard looked at Small One and laughed. "I know a man who is in need of such an animal," he said. "Go to the third shop inside these gates."

"Oh, thank you, sir," said the boy.

The boy and Small One found the shop and went inside. It was very dark, and it smelled bad. Some other animals were tied up inside. They looked frightened.

"Now don't be afraid, Small One," said the boy.

They looked around. At first they did not see anyone. Then they saw a man sharpening a knife.

"Hello," called the boy.
The man came toward them.
"Yes?" he said.
The boy said nothing.
"Do you have a donkey to sell?" asked the man.
"Yes . . . his name is Small One," the boy replied.
"I will give you one piece of silver."

"Will you take good care of him?"

The man was surprised.

"I only want his hide, boy. I am a tanner."

"You want to make leather out of him!" the boy cried.

"One piece of silver," repeated the tanner.

"No, no, I won't sell him!" shouted the boy as he and Small One ran out of the shop.

The boy and the donkey ran through the streets. When they were far from the tanner's shop, they stopped to catch their breath.

"I'm sorry, Small One," said the boy. The little donkey licked him.

Small One and the boy walked through the marketplace. They saw a potter working at his wheel.

"Would you like to buy my donkey?" asked the boy.

"Not that sorry bag of bones," said the potter.

Then the boy saw a baker.

"Would you buy my donkey?" he asked.

"Not that scrawny little beast," said the baker. "Since my wife is so fat, I think I should buy a horse, at least."

"Doesn't anybody need a donkey?" the boy asked three merchants who were passing by.

"Take our advice," they said. "You will never find a buyer here. Go see the horse trader, three blocks straight ahead."

The boy took Small One over to the horse trader's stand. The trader was selling a beautiful horse for fifty pieces of silver.

"Please, sir, would you sell my donkey?" asked the boy as he led Small One up the ramp.

The man took a look at Small One and laughed and laughed. He decided to make fun of the little donkey.

"Look at this beautiful animal," he said to the crowd. "Who will pay one thousand pieces of silver for him?"

Everyone laughed.

"But you can see that he is as strong as a bull," the horse trader continued as he got on Small One's back.

At first the poor little donkey was almost flattened by the weight.

"Get off!" shouted the boy.

But then Small One gathered all his strength and tossed the man high into the air. The horse trader landed in a heap on the ground.

"Get that miserable beast out of here!" he shouted to the boy, who rushed away with the donkey.

Small One and the boy walked slowly through the streets. The tired donkey knew there was only one solution. He led the boy back to the tanner's shop, ready to give up his life to help the boy. They were both very sad. The boy sat down in the street and cried. He put his arms around Small One's neck. Suddenly he heard a man's voice.

"Tell me, son, are you the owner of this small donkey? I need a gentle animal to carry my wife, Mary, to Bethlehem. Is he for sale?"

The boy looked up at the man's friendly face.

"Yes, sir," he said.

"What do you call him?"

"Small One," replied the boy, smiling.

"Well, he looks strong enough."

"And kind," said the boy.

The man smiled. "I can offer you only one piece of silver," he said. "I know it is very little."

The boy felt he could trust the man. "Oh, that's fine!" he said. "I just want Small One to have a good home."

"Well, my son, he will," said the man, rubbing the donkey's head. "I will take good care of him." Then he gave the boy the piece of silver.

The boy gave his friend one last hug. "Good-bye, Small One. Be strong and sure of foot and follow your new master."

"Come along, Small One," said the man as he turned to go.

Then the little boy climbed high atop the town wall to wave good-bye to the man, his wife, and Small One as they began their journey to Bethlehem.

The boy felt sad and happy at the same time. He was certain that Small One would have a good life with his new family.